For further information on Enid Blyton
please contact www.blyton.com

ISBN 0-86163-994-4

First published 1952 by Brockhampton Press Limited in
*Enid Blyton's Bright Story Book*
This edition first published 1984
Re-issued 1999

Published by Award Publications Limited,
27 Longford Street, London NW1 3DZ

Printed in India

# Enid Blyton

# THE WISHING FEATHER

## Illustrated by Suzy-Jane Tanner

AWARD PUBLICATIONS LIMITED

One day, when Snubby was walking along the road, he saw a pretty blue feather lying in the gutter. It had a red tip to it and Snubby liked it.

"Just the thing to stick in my hat," he said and he picked up the feather and stuck it into his hat. He at once felt very grand indeed and went whistling along the road. He didn't know that it was a wishing feather!

He passed by Dame Cooky's little shop. The plump old dame was just setting out some hot pasties in her little window. They did look nice.

"Look at those!" said Snubby, stopping. "I do wish I had one to eat!"

Well, of course, as he had a wishing feather in his hat, his wish came true. He suddenly felt something hot against his side and he put his hand into his pocket in alarm to see what it was. In his pocket was a hot pasty! Well, well, of all the surprises! Snubby took it out and looked at it.

"I don't know where you came from, but I do know where you're going," he said, and took an enormous bite out of the pasty.

But it was very hot and he burned his tongue. He gave a howl that made Dame Cooky look up. She saw Snubby eating one of her pasties. Yes, there was no doubt about it at all! She counted them quickly and there was one missing.

Bad Snubby! Wicked Snubby!

She ran out of her little shop and snatched the pasty from Snubby's hand. He was most surprised and very cross indeed to see his lovely pasty being thrown down into the gutter and stamped on by Dame Cooky's big feet.

"You bad little thief!" shouted Dame Cooky. "Stealing one of my pasties and eating it under my very nose!"

"I didn't steal it! You nasty, horrid person!" cried Snubby. "I wish you were in your oven, cooking with your pasties, so there!"

Well, of course, Snubby still had that wishing feather in his cap and in a second Dame Cooky found herself

back in her kitchen – and, oh my, she was being
crammed into her hot oven with the next batch of her
pasties. How she yelled and screamed!

Mr Top-Hat, her next-door neighbour, ran to rescue
her and pulled her out of the oven at once.

"Do you want to cook yourself?" he said to her.
"Whatever are you trying to get into your oven for?
Pooh, you smell scorched."

"It's that wicked Snubby!" cried Dame Cooky, and she
ran out into the road again. "He wished me in my oven
– and there I was! He's got hold of some magic
somehow. We'd better catch him before he uses it on
us all!"

Mr Top-Hat and Dame Cooky pounced on Snubby and shook him hard. "Where's the magic you are using?" they cried. "Give it up at once!"

Shake, shake, shake! Snubby's teeth rattled in his head and his eyes nearly fell out.

"I haven't any magic!" he gasped. "I haven't, I haven't. Let me go! Take your hands off me! I wish you hadn't got any, you horrid things!" In an instant Mr Top-Hat and Dame Cooky let go of Snubby – and, oh dear, they had paws instead of hands! Snubby's wish had come true. He stared at the paws and so did they.

"My wishes are coming true," said Snubby, in a loud voice. "I don't know why. But they are. I'm powerful! I'm important! I'm grand!"

"Wish our hands back again!" said poor Dame Cooky, weeping. "How am I to make pasties with paws like these? Wish our hands back again."

"Certainly not," said Snubby. "It serves you both right. My word, what a time I shall have, paying people back for horrid things they've done to me!"

"Wouldn't it be better to forget all that and pay people back for the good turns they have done you?" said Mr Top-Hat. "When you have a bit of power, you want to do good, not bad, Snubby. Be careful or you will be sorry."

"Pooh!" said Snubby. "You only say that because you want me to wish you back your hands. Well, I shan't. I'm going to enjoy myself now. Hello, here comes Mr Smack. Many a time he's spanked me. I'll wish him a few things to wake him up a bit!"

Mr Smack came nearer. He was the village schoolmaster, a learned and strict old fellow. Snubby let out a yell as he came up.

"Hello, Smack! I wish you had a cane running behind you to make you hurry!"

In no time at all, a long thin cane appeared behind poor Mr Smack and hit him very smartly indeed. Mr Smack yelled and began to run. The cane hopped along, too, getting in a good old smack every now and again.

Snubby jumped about for joy. "Now I wish a whip would come and crack round his ears!" he shouted.

The whip appeared, and what with its loud cracking and the whippy little cane, poor Mr Smack had a very bad time indeed.

Then up came Dame Tick-Tock and Father Bent. Snubby greeted them with a loud shout.

"You scolded me the other day! Now I'll pay you back! You've got your best clothes on and I wish you'd get wet through!"

Down came a shower of rain, right over the poor surprised Dame Tick-Tock and Father Bent. How wet they were! It was a most surprising sight, really, because no rain fell anywhere except over the two astonished people.

Soon the word went round that Snubby had got hold of some wishing-magic and was using it. Everyone came running to see what was happening. When they saw Dame Cooky and Mr Top-Hat with paws instead of hands, and saw poor Mr Smack trying to escape from the cane and the whip, and Dame Tick-Tock and Father Bent getting wetter and wetter, they were amazed.

"Now stop this, Snubby!" cried Mr Plod the policeman. "How dare you behave like this? I'll take you to the police station and lock you up."

Snubby roared with laughter. "I wish a dozen policemen would run after you and try to catch you to take you to the police station!" he said.

Suddenly twelve big policemen appeared and went to put heavy hands on the astonished Mr Plod. He began to struggle with them and got away. They ran after him. Snubby laughed till the tears ran down his cheeks.

Then people began to feel afraid. Snubby certainly had got some kind of powerful wishing-magic; there was no doubt about it. And he was using it badly. There was no knowing what might happen if power was in the hands of a bad pixie who didn't know how to use it.

One by one the watching people crept away, afraid of Snubby and scared of what he might do to them. Snubby saw them going, and he rejoiced to see how frightened everyone looked.

"Come back!" he shouted, and a great idea came into his head. "Come back! I want to tell you something. I am very great and powerful now. I can wish for anything I want. I am the most important person in the whole of this town. I shall be your king."

"You are not fit to be a king," said Mr Smack, dodging the whip that cracked around his ears. "A king should know how to use power rightly and well. You don't. And you never will."

"I wish for six canes behind you!" shouted Snubby in anger. "Aha! They will make you jump. How dare you talk to me like that."

Everyone was silent. Snubby threw out his chest and strutted up and down. "I am your king. I shall have a grand golden carriage. I wish for it now, drawn by twelve black horses!"

It came, of course. One minute it wasn't there and the next it was, a fine gleaming carriage with twelve black horses that pawed the ground impatiently. Snubby climbed into it and sat himself down, folding his arms.

"I wish for a coachman and two footmen!" he said, and hey presto! There they were.

"Now I wish for a golden palace with a thousand windows," shouted Snubby, feeling tremendously excited. There was a loud gasp as the watching crowd saw a beautiful palace appear on the hill nearby. Its thousand windows glittered in the sun.

Snubby gave a shout of joy. "See that?" he yelled. "That's my home! And I'm your king! Bow down to me, all of you! Bow down or I'll turn you into black-beetles!"

Everyone except Mr Smack at once bowed themselves low to the ground. Only Mr Smack stood upright and the cane gave him a horrid little smack. Snubby pointed his finger at Mr Smack, who had suddenly caught sight of the wishing feather in the pixie's hat.

"Yes, there is no doubt about it," thought the surprised Mr Smack, "that is a wishing feather!" How had Snubby got hold of it? And did he know he had it? The cane gave him a swipe on the legs and made him jump.

"Hey, you!" roared Snubby, still pointing his finger at Mr Smack. "Bow down to me, do you hear? I'm your king."

An idea flashed into Mr Smack's quick mind. "You are not a king till you wear a cloak and a crown," he said. "Where is your crown?"

"That's easy!" cried Snubby. "I wish for a cloak and fine clothes, and I wish for a golden crown!"

Away flew his old clothes and in their stead came gleaming ones of red and silver. Away flew his hat and on his head came a glittering crown. "Now I am your king!" cried Snubby to Mr Smack. "Bow down!"

Mr Smack did not bow down. He watched the hat whisk away with the wishing feather in it. He knew what would happen when that was gone. All Snubby's magic would go. Ho, ho! What a shock for Snubby!

"If you don't bow down at once, I'll wish you a pair of donkey's ears!" cried Snubby in a rage, pointing his finger at Mr Smack again. "What, you won't bow? Then I wish you had donkey's ears on your head!"

But no donkey's ears came. And suddenly everything began to change. The gleaming palace on the hill faded into a mist and all its thousand windows were gone. The lovely carriage faded, too, and Snubby found himself tumbling to the ground. The horses threw up their heads, neighed, and disappeared. The coachmen and footmen vanished.

Dame Cooky's hands
came back and so did Mr
Top-Hat's. Dame Tick-Tock
and Father Bent were no
longer wet through. The
twelve policemen, who
were after Mr Plod, faded away like shadows in the sun.

All Snubby's fine clothes disappeared and his crown
as well. But his old clothes didn't come back, nor did
his hat with the lovely wishing feather. There stood
poor Snubby in his holey vest and nothing else,
shivering and scared. The wishing feather was gone and
his wishes would no longer come true. He could do no
more magic. He had used it so badly; and now this was
his punishment. "All my magic is gone!" he wailed.
"There's nothing left."

16

But there was something left – and that was the nasty little cane that had first come to annoy Mr Smack. That hadn't gone – and now it left Mr Smack and came hopping over to Snubby. *Whee!* It gave him a fine blow and made him jump in the air! *Whee!*

"Don't, don't!" cried Snubby, and fled away. But the little whippy cane followed him and everyone laughed to see Snubby leap into the air every time he was hit.

"He could have wished a thousand good wishes," said Mr Smack. "Now all that is left to him is one bad one. Ah, if only I had found that wishing feather, what a wonderful lot of good I'd have done with it!"

It was a waste, wasn't it?